POPO
THE ADVENTURES OF A
MEXICAN DONKEY

This is the story of Popo, a friendly Mexican donkey. He is so eager to see the world beyond his village, and so entranced with the idea of adventure, that one day he leaves home and goes off with a passing donkey train.

Popo is an endearing hero, whose adventures provide true-life pictures of Mexico and some interesting and amusing "donkey's eye" views of life in general and people in particular. This little donkey will win reader's hearts through his discovery that life has its rewards for the stout heart and gentle nature.

Dr. William R. Strieber is a Maryland veterinarian. He has traveled to several countries for the United Nations Relief and Rehabilitation Organization, treating horses aboard ship, and he has spent five years in remote regions of Mexico caring for animals. *Popo* expresses his special closeness to the people and life of Mexico as well as his love for animals.

Flora M. Rizzotto, who lives in New Mexico, is a graduate of the Palmer Institute of Authorship and winner of the 1967 *Wick Magazine* award for poetry. She has a warm affinity for the Spanish-speaking people of Mexico and the Southwest.

Gladys Ely, whose charming illustrations appear in this book, is a graduate of the Fine Arts Department of the University of Nebraska and the Chicago Art Institute. She has had a varied art career, teaching and illustrating publications, both for adults and children. She has made frequent visits to Mexico and says the burros are very dear to her.

POPO

THE ADVENTURES OF A MEXICAN DONKEY

by

William R. Strieber
and
Flora M. Rizzotto

illustrated by
Gladys Ely

A QUEST Book for Children

Published under a grant from The Kern Foundation

THE THEOSOPHICAL PUBLISHING HOUSE
Wheaton, Ill., U.S.A.
Madras, India/London, England

© Copyright The Theosophical Publishing House 1971
All rights reserved

The Theosophical Publishing House, Wheaton, Illinois, is a department of
The Theosophical Society in America

ISBN: 0-8356-0420-9
Library of Congress Catalog Number 70-146604
Manufactured in the United States of America

The authors wish to acknowledge the inspirational encouragement of Shirley Strieber, and the typing hours she contributed, during the preliminary drafting of the manuscript of this book.

CONTENTS

Chapter 1

Adventure Underfoot

Popo stood as tall on his four short legs as he possibly could.

"I want to see what the mountains are like," he said to his mother. "I want to follow the river and see where it goes."

The little brown donkey was fuzzy-haired and wide-awake, with brown fearless eyes. He and his mother lived in Mexico, in a small adobe village away from the large, busy cities.

"If you left home, who would help me take Don Pancho's sugar cane to the mill?" Popo's mother replied. "Who would give you shelter, food and water

1

when you are far away among strangers?" she asked. "It is best to stay at home," she advised, and she smiled and wiggled her ears and wrinkled her nose.

Popo stretched out his neck and looked long and far, from one side of the horizon to the other side.

"Hee-haw! I am not afraid," the brown donkey said. "Hee-haw! I am not afraid."

Popo was a very brave little donkey, and that was why Don Pancho had named him after a great Mexican warrior of ancient times. A wonderful volcano that overlooks the majestic capital city of Mexico is also named after this gallant, legendary hero.

"I'll travel and see the world," Popo told his mother. "I'll follow the green river that goes by the red clay village," he murmured in a low, low voice, as if he were singing to himself.

"I'll go right through the green and yellow sugar cane fields, and travel and travel until I reach the misty blue mountains," Popo continued to himself.

It was from the river that Don Pancho watered his sugar cane fields. Popo's mother lowered her head every moment or so to nibble at some sweet, tender grass. She just looked wise and said nothing more.

It was a very fine morning for thinking of one's heart's desires, and Popo dreamed his dreams, as he looked at the long line of blue mountains that filled part of the sky behind the mysterious approach of the river.

"I shall follow the winding river and go to see for myself what the mountains are like," Popo declared again, as though to the air, and to the grass, and to the trees, rather than to his mother, who now was eating some straw a few feet away. Little did Popo know how very soon his heart's desire was to come true in his life!

During the noon siesta, or the time of rest during the heat of the day in Mexico, Popo and his mother were

standing in the shade of Don Pancho's house. They were flicking flies from their backs with their brush-like tails when they saw a great cloud of dust moving toward them.

"It's a donkey train," Popo's mother said, as she looked with experienced eyes at the ribbon of dust.

"What's a donkey train?" Popo asked, and his dark eyes gleamed with interest.

"It's a train of donkeys who carry loads of sugar, salt, coffee and other things from village to village," she explained.

Don Pancho came out of the house to greet the owner of the train, who was a tall man with a serious but kind face.

"We have been delayed on the trail because one of my donkeys is lame," he said to Don Pancho. "May I stop here a while and rest in the shade?"

"Of course, of course," Don Pancho welcomed him. He enjoyed receiving guests, even strangers, as they always brought news from other places.

Popo was overcome with curiosity, and he went over to investigate the nine strange donkeys. He sniffed noses with a big, reddish-colored donkey who was the leader of the train. All the donkeys had packs tied to their backs.

3

"Where are you going?" Popo asked the red-colored donkey. The strange donkey, whose name was Red, was pleased that Popo had recognized him as the leader of the train, and he answered with dignified courtesy.

"We are taking salt and coffee to a village. It will take us several days to reach it," he said. To Popo, the red donkey seemed to be all that he himself wanted to be—an important donkey who has had many adventures and who has traveled and seen the world.

Popo now saw a black donkey who was limping. He was the donkey who had delayed the train.

"What's wrong with him?" he asked Red.

"He cut his leg on a sharp rock," the leader donkey told him.

Popo was instantly sorry for the injured donkey who was no larger than himself.

"Does it hurt much?" he asked the black donkey with concern.

"Yes. I don't think I can go much farther," the black donkey admitted.

"I wish I could take your place, and you could stay here and rest," Popo said quickly, without really thinking about the matter very deeply.

Popo really wanted to have an adventure and to see the village where the donkey train was going, as well as to help the injured donkey.

He pricked up his ears as he listened to hear what Don Carlos, the owner of the donkey train, was saying to Don Pancho, his master.

"I'll leave you the lame black donkey, who will soon be well after he has a little rest, and buy that old, brown donkey from you," he bargained with Don Pancho, pointing at Popo.

"Old brown donkey!!!" Don Pancho replied quickly in a loud, angry voice. He was upset because Don

4

Carlos had slighted Popo. The little donkey was the "apple of his eye," and he felt as though he himself had been insulted.

"Popo is not yet two years old and too young for heavy work. Besides, he's the best donkey in my village," Don Pancho said, with warmth in his voice.

Popo's ears stood straight up, and he strutted up and down in front of the donkey train as though to say, "Hear that?"

Like most villagers, Don Pancho valued and took pride in his donkeys. There are many far-away places in the steep, tall mountains of Mexico that cannot be reached except on foot. In some of the dense jungles, there are roads that are as difficult to travel as the remote mountain trails. No matter how steep or dangerous the path, the trusty Mexican donkey could always be relied on to go anywhere his master could go.

Don Carlos was not at all bothered by Don Pancho's anger. He knew that an angry man often said things to be regretted later. "I'll give you five dollars and the little black donkey for Popo," he offered.

Don Pancho was more scornful than ever. "I wouldn't sell Popo for less than ten dollars," he said, hoping to impress the other man with Popo's worth and never dreaming that the other man could afford to pay that much.

"Sold!" Don Carlos replied, and his face was seamed all over with smile lines from his forehead to his lips. He knew he had made a good bargain.

"Here's your ten dollars and the black donkey," he said, still smiling broadly in his good fortune at buying the sturdy, stout-hearted Popo.

Popo's heart pounded in his strong little chest. In less time than it takes to tell, he had been sold! He had a new master, and soon he would have a new life.

The little donkey didn't know whether he was happy or sad. He realized with a sinking heart that his mother couldn't go with him.

Oh, how fast things can change, he thought to himself. But he lifted his head and said good-by to Don Pancho and his mother.

"Hee-haw! Hee-haw! Good-by, Don Pancho."

"Hee-haw! Hee-haw! Good-by, Mother. I'll be back to tell you all about the world." Popo said the words firmly, but inside of him he felt very shaky and unsure of everything . . . as though the world had just turned upside down.

"Hee-haw! Hee-haw! Good-by, Popo," his mother answered sadly, and Popo disappeared with Don Carlos and the donkey train around a bend in the long, long trail. Soon nothing was left to see of them but a large puff of dust.

Chapter 2

The Life of the Donkey Train

The pack on Popo's back was uncomfortable, but he was so interested to see the new and strange country-side he was traveling through he paid little attention to his burden. But later in the afternoon, the bags of salt he was carrying seemed to grow heavier and heavier.

"My back feels like it's breaking," he complained, and he began to shuffle along the dusty trail with weary, aching legs. Soon, he was lagging toward the rear of the train, and then he stopped to nibble some coarse green grass beside the road.

Crunch! Crunch! Crunch! Popo took three big bites. Crack!

"Hee-haw! Hee-haw" Popo cried, surprised by the sound of the crack of a rope popping near his left haunch.

Popo was alarmed by the sound, and he ran quickly to catch up with the other donkeys. As he ran, he looked back over his shoulder, and he saw Don Carlos holding a long rope.

Don Carlos soon caught up with the donkey train. His face was still and stern, but he never showed any anger or said a word to Popo. At heart, he was a very understanding man.

Popo was puzzled. When he had carried sugar cane on his back, Don Pancho had never minded if he wanted to stop a moment to munch a little grass. He didn't realize that Don Pancho had spoiled him. He didn't know that there is a right time for everything, even work and play, and that they were both personal responsibilities.

Late that afternoon, as the sun was setting in a deep pool of orange and gold sky, Don Carlos stopped the donkey train in a tiny village to spend the night.

Don Carlos paid a man to let him put the donkeys in a little field surrounded with a white rock fence. He removed the donkeys' packs for the night. Although there was some grass in the field, Don Carlos also bought a small bale of grass because he knew that working donkeys must have sufficient food for strength and endurance. He gave them some water, and then after eating a simple meal taken from his own personal supplies, he spread out his great brown poncho as a blanket and lay down on the ground to sleep under the stars.

Popo was unhappy. He was stiff and sore in every one of his small joints. He decided that he would run away and go back to Don Pancho and his mother. He knew that he could jump over the rock fence if he tried hard enough. And so he did!

Swish! Popo was startled and surprised to find a rope around his neck. Wise Don Carlos had expected Popo to run away and had quietly left his bed in order to watch him.

"Hee-haw! I'm caught already," Popo snorted in donkey fashion. He pulled at the rope, but that hurt his neck . . . he bucked . . . he tore up the ground with his hoofs . . . but the rope held fast!

Don Carlos took Popo back into the little field and tied his two front legs together with a short length of rope. Popo could still move about, but he couldn't jump or run.

I'll wait a while before I try to run away again, he decided. And so Popo settled down to the ways and life of the donkey train, but only temporarily—he thought to himself.

Late in the afternoon, two days later, they reached a large town where the contents of their packs were delivered to various merchants. The smell of the sun-baked clay of the adobe homes reminded Popo of his own little village, and he was homesick; but with his great sense for adventure and with his great love of life, he could never stay homesick for very long at a time.

Popo's muscles and legs no longer hurt him, for he was fast becoming accustomed to the working life of a donkey train. Don Carlos put the donkeys in a small pen with a cow and a calf who belonged to the owner of the pen. He tied Popo to the little calf because he knew that Popo might still try to run away.

"Look at me!" Popo exclaimed. "Tied to a calf! This is terrible. I'm no calf! I'm a donkey!"

"Ma-a-a-a!" said the calf. "Who wants to be a donkey?"

As soon as it was dark, Popo chewed the rope until

he was free. He kicked up his heels and jumped over the fence.

"Good-by, Red," he called back to the leader donkey. "I'm going home."

Clippity clop! Clippity clop! Popo trotted off through the dark village, feeling gay and pleased with himself.

As he rounded the corner of a house, he smelled corn, and he stopped as though he had applied an invisible set of brakes within himself. There was a large pile of corn in the yard.

"Oh, how I love corn," Popo said to no one in particular, and he began to eat the corn.

Crunch! Crunch! Crunch!

Smack! Smack! Smack! The corn was delicious.

And then, from behind, someone took a firm hold of Popo's two long ears. It was the owner of the corn! Popo could not pull away though he struggled and tried. He could not bite because his mouth was still full of corn.

"Hee-haw! I'm caught again," he said with disgust.

The owner of the corn put Popo in a small wire pen. He wanted to get his money from Popo's owner for the corn the brown donkey had eaten.

There were three donkeys in the pen, and they did not like strangers. One of them kicked Popo.

"Hee-haw! Ouch!" Popo cried. "What's the matter? Why do you kick me?"

"We don't like strangers who eat our corn and then sleep in our pen," replied the donkey who had kicked him.

Popo ran to a corner of the pen, turned his tail toward the other donkeys, and kept his hind feet ready to kick, if necessary. He didn't sleep well that night.

The next morning Don Carlos found Popo and paid

11

the owner of the corn for the corn that Popo had eaten. He scowled at Popo.

"You greedy donkey! I'll have to watch you more closely." He put a rope around Popo's neck and led him back to the donkey train.

Don Carlos loaded the donkeys with packs of brightly colored blankets that he had bought. In this town the people were known far and wide for their skillful weaving and dyeing of fine woolen blankets. They raised their own sheep and cut the sheep's wool for the blankets that they wove and sold.

Red was not surprised to see Popo, and he teased him a little.

"Well! Well! I thought you'd be well on your way back home by now."

Popo didn't answer. He knew that he had made a mistake.

Don Carlos did not load Popo with a pack. Instead, he threw a bright red blanket over his sturdy back and got on Popo's back himself.

"I'll just ride instead of walking," he said in a dry tone of voice. "I can keep a closer watch on you this way."

Popo was indignant with this turn of events. He tried to bite and then to throw Don Carlos off his back. But Don Carlos was too clever for him and never moved an inch.

"Hee-haw! Watch me brush Don Carlos off," he said to Red who was watching closely to see what Don Carlos would do with the rebellious Popo. Popo headed for a tall clump of sticker bushes, thinking to brush Don Carlos against the giant sized stickers.

Red just smiled because he knew that Don Carlos was a lot smarter than a mere donkey.

Don Carlos refused to budge from Popo's back.

Soon Popo realized that Don Carlos was truly his master and ceased to fight. He had learned that neither running away, nor stealing, nor fighting was the answer to getting his freedom back.

Chapter 3

The Rise and Fall of a Hero

It had been a long, hot day on the road for the donkey train, but now the sun was setting in a great ball of flaming red and gold, and the white clouds in the sky were turning to deep shades of blue and purple.

Don Carlos halted the donkeys beside a little spring of running water. There was no village in sight, just some rocks and low bushes and a few trees. The air was fast becoming cold without the warmth of the sun.

"Why are we stopping here?" Popo asked in surprise.

"Because it's getting dark and the next village is far away," Red told him.

Don Carlos unloaded the donkeys and immediately they all stretched their legs and then lay down on the ground to roll over and over until they felt better after

15

having the heavy packs on their backs all day.

The donkeys drank from the spring and began to eat the grass that grew around it. Don Carlos tied together the front legs of each donkey with a short length of rope so they couldn't wander far from camp.

All was quiet except for some chirping crickets and the munching of the donkeys. Don Carlos built a fire to cook his supper and sat down to eat. After he finished eating, his head began to nod and soon he dozed off to sleep.

Popo was eating clumps of grass as fast as he could when suddenly a dead tree limb snapped with a loud crack.

As he jerked his head up to listen, two robbers sprang out of the dark bushes and jumped on the dozing Don Carlos. Don Carlos instantly threw off one of the robbers and knocked the other one down directly in front of Popo.

The first robber threw himself back on Don Carlos, and they struggled and fought each other. The second robber that Don Carlos had knocked down in front of Popo reached for a large stick. He was going to hit the tall and strong Don Carlos over the head with it.

Popo saw at once what the villain intended to do, and when he bent over to pick up the stick, Popo, who was just itching to kick something anyway, turned and kicked him hard with his hind feet. He kicked the robber right into the campfire.

Wham! Crash! Yeow!

Frightened and burned, the would-be bandit scrambled out of the scattered campfire and ran away into the night. When his partner, who was receiving a good beating from Don Carlos, saw this, he too took to his heels and ran away as though a ghost were after him.

Don Carlos dipped his handkerchief into the cool

spring water and bathed his cut and bruised face.

"You are a brave donkey, Popo. You have helped me save the donkey train and all its supplies and goods," he said gratefully.

As a special thank-you treat, Don Carlos gave Popo some corn he had been saving. All the donkeys told Popo that he was a hero, and Popo was very proud of himself.

The next morning, before the sun's great rays of light had reached the top of the mountains, the donkey train was on its way again. Don Carlos did not ride Popo; instead he put a fairly light pack of bright colored blankets on his back.

"You look very happy this morning, Popo," Red said to him.

"I am happy!" Popo admitted. "It won't be long now before I'll see my mother and Don Pancho again."

"Oh, we aren't going back to your village now, Popo," Red told him. "We must make many trips to other villages before we pass back near your village again."

Seeing Popo's face become downcast, Red added with sympathy, "I'm sorry, Popo."

Popo's heart sank. He wanted to see the world, but now he was homesick again, and it would have been great fun to return home now that he was a hero.

Red tried to cheer him up. "Don't be sad, Popo. There are many interesting things to see in the village where we are taking these blankets."

But Popo didn't feel cheered. He shuffled sadly along, and he didn't even bother to switch his tail at the buzzing flies that lit on his back.

At noon they arrived in a village where there was much excitement and activity. At noontime, the village square was usually quiet with the men of the town dozing in the shade.

17

But now the village band was playing merrily and the people were laughing and talking. It was market day. One day each week all the people from the farms and smaller villages around came to buy and sell chickens, eggs, vegetables, corn, cheese, baskets and clay pots. It was the happiest day of the week.

"Listen to the music," Popo exclaimed, perking up at once. He loved to hear gay music.

Many people crowded around the colorful donkey train with its bright red, blue and green blankets. Popo's spirits rose as he marched gayly behind Red, keeping in step with the band music.

"Just look at those fine donkeys," Popo heard someone say, and his ears stood up straighter and he switched his tail in time with the music.

Don Carlos promised a small barefoot boy some candy if he would watch the donkey train while he visited some friends. He left the donkeys in the shade of a very large tree, and they stood and dozed, content and happy to rest in the shade. The boy, who was supposed to be watching the donkeys, also fell fast asleep.

But Popo didn't sleep. He was thirsty, and his restlessness kept Red from taking a nap. Although Red told Popo he had best stay there and out of trouble, Popo decided to go across the street to get a drink from a water trough. He couldn't see any harm in doing that.

But after getting a drink, Popo became hungry. He sniffed around on the ground, nibbling here and there and slowly moved farther and farther away from the donkey train.

He saw a line of clothes drying in the sun behind a small house, and the clothes looked tempting to Popo. He reached up, craning his neck, so he could have a bite.

Gulp! He swallowed a little shirt whole. Next he ate a large red handkerchief. That was better than the

19

shirt, he thought to himself, and then he ate a bright green dress.

Whack! Whack! Whack!

"Hee-haw! Ouch!" Popo cried, as an angry woman hit him again and again over his head with her broom.

"Get out of my yard," she screamed at Popo.

Whack! Whack! Whack! Popo ran as fast as he could to get away from the angry woman.

When he arrived back at the donkey train, Don Carlos was there.

"Where have you been, Popo?" he asked in a scolding tone of voice.

Popo hung his head. A piece of green dress was still in one corner of his mouth. Just then, the angry woman came running up.

"Your donkey ate five of my shirts, six dresses and eight big handkerchiefs—and you owe me ten dollars for them," she shouted at Don Carlos before he could even say a word.

"I don't have that much money," Don Carlos replied at once and looked with reproach in his eyes at the now conscience-stricken Popo.

"Then I'll call the police and have you arrested," she cried, getting more and more angry, although she knew that Popo hadn't actually eaten that many of her clothes.

"Help! Police! Police!" the woman shrieked at the top of her lungs.

"Wait! Wait!" Don Carlos pleaded. "I'll pay."

The woman stopped screaming.

"Will you take something worth ten dollars?" Don Carlos asked.

"What?" the woman asked suspiciously.

"This fine donkey . . . Popo!" he said, as though he was offering the woman a very fine bargain indeed.

"What? And have him eat me out of house and home?" she said tartly. And she opened her mouth to yell "Pol-e-e-e-ce!" all over again.

"Wait! Wait! Take my last five dollars," Don Carlos offered in desperation. He didn't want to get into trouble with the police.

The woman snatched the money out of Don Carlos's hand and went home satisifed.

"Shame on you, Popo," Red said, and all the other donkeys shook their heads in agreement. No one remembered any more that Popo had been a hero.

"Oh, how unlucky I am," Popo sighed.

"Oh no, not luck," Red disagreed. "If you had thought about what you were doing before you did it, you wouldn't have gotten into trouble," he said wisely.

Popo knew that this was true, and he was sorry for what he had done. He was sorry he had caused Don Carlos both distress and a loss of money.

Chapter 4

Popo Receives a Title

Popo had never seen the mountains look so near and large before. Although they were still a great distance away, they loomed with majestic outlines across the deep yellow horizon. It was late afternoon, and from the top of a very steep hill, Popo could see a pink adobe village below that was splashed with rose and gold shadows.

The hill was of clay covered with loose rock that was sharp and slick like glass underfoot.

"Be careful, Popo," Red warned him. "Many donkeys have fallen down this hill, and some have broken their legs."

"Careful now," Don Carlos said in a quiet soothing tone of voice to the donkeys.

Popo concentrated on the steep descent. He slipped

once, but Don Carlos steadied him with a strong hand.

At last, at the bottom of the dangerous hill, Popo breathed a sigh of relief, and he admired Red's and the other donkeys' serene, sure-footed ability. He knew that their packs were much heavier than his.

In the glowing pink village, Don Carlos made arrangements for the donkeys to spend the night in a big stable that had thick walls made of red-pink clay mixed with yellow straw. There was no roof over the walls, but there were two wooden sheds inside with no sides.

It was still early evening, but the donkeys were all tired, and as soon as they had finished eating they settled down to sleep.

Bang! Bang! Bang!

Popo jumped up. "What was that?" he asked in alarm. He had never heard such loud sounds before.

All the donkeys hee-hawed and complained that Popo had waked them up. They knew what the noise was and it didn't bother them at all.

Bang! Bang! Bang! Popo didn't know what the noise was, and it bothered him.

"Settle down, Popo," Red said. "It's just fireworks. The people here love firecrackers and rockets so they make their own. They like to hear the loud noises and to see the skyrockets shooting up in the dark."

Red looked up at the sky as he said this. "Look!" he said to Popo. "See the colors and lights in the sky?"

Popo looked but he still didn't like the noise.

"I won't be able to sleep a wink tonight," he grumbled.

Red laughed. "The rest of us will sleep. We don't mind the sound of firecrackers at all."

All the donkeys went back to sleep—all except Popo. He wished the noise would stop.

Swoosh!

Popo could see a fiery skyrocket zoom through the air with red, blue and yellow sparks trailing behind. In spite of himself, he couldn't help enjoying the beautiful colors streaming through the black sky.

Popo's eyelids drooped, and he was just dropping off to sleep when his nose started to tickle.

"Ka-chew! Ka-chew!" he sneezed.

Popo sniffed and then jumped up. He smelled smoke, and it wasn't just the smell of fireworks. He saw that a skyrocket had landed in the dry hay and that the stable was on fire.

"Get up, Red! Get up everyone!" Popo shouted. "Hee-haw! Hee-haw! Fire! Fire!"

Immediately, the other donkeys were awake. They ran back and forth and round and round the enclosure of the stable. There was no way out. The fire burned brighter and brighter but no help came.

"We must get out," Red cried, and he hee-hawed as loud as he could, hoping to attract the attention of someone who would let them out. The donkeys milled around in a panic of fear.

"We are lost!" they wailed to each other.

Popo forced himself to stand still so he could think. He twitched his ears in thought. He had an idea. He ran over to the locked stable door.

Bam! Bam! Bam! He kicked the door with all the strength in his hind feet and legs. Someone will hear me kicking, he said to himself.

The donkeys coughed and coughed as the fire burned higher and higher and the smoke became thicker and thicker.

Popo knew that it would be too late if they didn't get out of the burning, smoke-filled stables at once. With his last bit of strength, he kicked the stable door harder than he had ever kicked anything in his life.

Bang! Whang! The door came crashing down.

"Follow me!" Popo shouted.

Red, remembering his duty as the leader of the donkeys, quickly ran around the stable dodging the flames as best he could in order to see that all the donkeys followed Popo out the now opened door.

Popo had kicked the stable door down just as Don Carlos and some men came running up the street. Many people were running toward the stable with buckets of water to put the fire out.

Popo was a hero again! The people fed him corn and lumps of sugar. They hung a big garland of flowers around his neck and paraded him around the village square.

People called out, "What a smart, brave donkey! Brave donkey! Well done!" Many wanted to buy Popo.

"Don Carlos! I'll give you fifteen dollars for Popo," called one man.

"I'll give you eighteen," offered another.

"Twenty!" cried a third.

Don Carlos silenced the crowd of people by holding up his hands. He stepped up on a big box and everyone grew quiet when they saw that he was going to give a speech.

"Good friends, Popo, and faithful donkeys!" he said in a loud voice. "It is a great honor for me to own such fine donkeys. No, I wouldn't sell one hair of any of my donkeys! Popo has cost me a little money in the past, it is true; however, tonight he has not only saved the lives of all the donkeys, but he has saved me from becoming a poor man as well.

"And it isn't the first time he has done me this service," he told the people. Don Carlos then told them how Popo had run off one of the two would-be robbers just a short time before, and how, when the other robber

DON POPO

had seen this, he had become frightened and had fled also.

"From now on, we will call Popo, Don Popo," Don Carlos announced with great eloquence. This meant that Popo was now a very distinguished donkey. "Three cheers for Don Popo!" he shouted.

"Hurrah! Hurrah! Hurrah!" the people shouted.

"Hee-haw! Hee-haw! Hee-haw!" brayed all the donkeys.

Don Popo pranced up and down. He held his ears up straight. When everyone was quiet, he went "Hee-haw! Hee-haw! Hee-haw!" and everyone clapped their hands.

"Silence! Silence!" Don Carlos shouted, again holding up his hands. "Don Popo deserves a reward for his bravery and for being so smart," he said.

"Let's give him corn," one man said.

"Let's give him green hay," shouted another.

"No," Don Carlos said. "There's something better than that. I'll take him back to his village and to his former owner, Don Pancho, just as soon as we deliver these blankets."

"Hurrah! Hurrah! the people shouted again.

"Hee-haw! Hee-haw!" brayed the donkeys over and over.

After Don Carlos found another stable for them, all the donkeys went back to sleep and slept soundly the night through, including Don Popo, who was now a very happy donkey.

Chapter 5

Ramón the Donkey Thief

When Don Carlos and the donkey train left the village, the people came out to wave good-by to Popo, and he was given a fresh garland of flowers. The people called out, "Good-by, Don Popo."

It was a bright, sunny morning and Popo stepped high as he walked. He was very proud of his new title. Don Carlos waved his big hat at the people, and all the donkeys bowed to the left and to the right.

Little did Popo dream that his glory was to be very short-lived and that destiny had many fresh surprises in store for him before he would be permitted to return to Don Pancho and the village where he had been born.

All the donkeys were in high spirits, and they made very good time that day. They arrived early in the afternoon in a town where Don Carlos sold his blankets for a very good price.

"Well, my fine friends," Don Carlos said to the donkeys, "let's get you some good corn and some alfalfa hay. You certainly deserve it." Alfalfa hay was the favorite hay of the donkeys because it was very flavorful and tasty.

When they arrived at the stable where Don Carlos was accustomed to take his donkeys, the stable was already filled up and there was no room for them. Don Carlos found room at another stable near the edge of the town, but he wasn't happy about leaving his donkeys in this strange place, because he couldn't get a room to stay nearby.

He didn't know the owner of the stable, so he stayed long enough to make sure that the donkeys were given plenty of alfalfa hay, corn and water. The owner of this stable assured Don Carlos that he slept next door and that the donkeys would be safe. So Don Carlos went back into the little town to find a place to eat and a room where he could sleep.

Before dark, the owner of the stable checked on the donkeys, and seeing that everything was all right, decided that he would go into town for a while. He didn't think there could be any harm in that if he didn't stay too long. So off he went, and Popo and the rest of the donkeys were left alone.

Shortly after the stable owner left, a sly-faced man with a large mustache opened the stable door cautiously. He stood quiet for a moment and looked around. He had seen the owner of the place leave, and he was making sure that there was no one else around. He was Ramón the donkey thief.

Satisifed that there was no one else there, Ramón went back for his horse which he had left in the shadows on another side of the stable. Leading his horse, he now went boldly into the stable and took a quick but professional look at all the donkeys. He wanted to pick out the best donkey, but he also wanted to be quick. He knew that the owner of the stable wouldn't be gone for long.

"Ah! There's the best donkey," Ramón said quietly to himself, as his greedy eyes lit on Popo. Quickly, he threw a rope with expert ease over Popo's neck.

"Nice donkey, come on," he coaxed.

Popo was not fooled. He didn't like the looks of this man at all. He planted all four of his feet firmly on the ground and refused to budge.

"Well, then, I'll fix you," Ramón muttered harshly, and he jumped upon his horse. He tied the rope he had thrown around Popo's neck to his saddle and started dragging the reluctant donkey by sheer horse power.

Popo was forced to follow, otherwise the rope around his neck would tighten so he couldn't breathe.

"Hee-haw! Hee-haw!" Popo cried, but no one was near enough to hear him or the other donkeys, who were braying loudly now that they saw Popo being dragged out of the stable.

Ramón was very smart as well as sly; he quickly left town with Popo, and they traveled all night, not stopping for food or drink. Ramón the donkey thief wanted to put as much distance as possible between himself and the police.

When they came to a wide river, they rode across on a ferryboat. Although Popo didn't know it, this was the very same river that flowed by his village and by Don Pancho's sugar cane fields so many miles away. After crossing the river, Ramón forced him to continue the mad flight.

Popo, needless to say, was very upset at this change in his fortune. Now, he would never see Don Pancho and his mother again, he thought to himself.

"Woe is me!" he sighed out loud. "I will miss Don Carlos and Red, too. But now I'll never see any of them again."

"Hee-haw! Hee-haw! Let me go. I want to go back to my friends," Popo brayed.

Ramón the thief laughed at Popo's discontent.

"Quiet!" he commanded and pulled hard on the rope around Popo's neck until Popo was forced to be quiet.

Back in the town where Popo had been stolen, Don Carlos had asked the police to help him find the little brown donkey. He even offered a reward of five dollars, but the police told him that it wasn't likely that they could ever find the thief who had been so sly and quick.

On the third day after Popo's abduction, Ramón and the sorrowful, brown donkey arrived at a village where the thief was not known, and Ramón sold Popo to the first man who was willing to pay the price that he asked for the stolen donkey. Since Popo was clearly a strong, husky and healthy young donkey, this was done very quickly.

And so, once again Popo had a new master and a new life.

Chapter 6

Troubles, Troubles Everywhere!

The man who bought Popo was an unpleasant, sour-faced man with a short temper. His name was Enrico, and he supplied the town of Rosa with milk and firewood. Rosa was in the foothills of the tall blue mountains. Not far to the south of Rosa were thick jungles and forests where only old and ancient ruins stood alongside a few tiny remote villages.

Enrico looked at Popo, who was dirty, tired and hungry. "What a good-for-nothing donkey you must be!" he said, ungraciously. "But I'll make sure that you earn your feed and keep," he promised in a hard voice and with a cruel glint in his eyes.

Whack! He hit Popo with a stick. "Get up, lazy-bones! Come along!"

Enrico put Popo in a small, dirty stable and gave him a few dry corn stalks to eat. Popo sadly finished the dry, tasteless food and drank the bucket of water in two long gulps. Although he was heartsick, he was so tired he fell asleep at once.

Whack! Whack! Whack!

"Get up, lazy donkey," said a harsh voice.

Popo jumped to his feet as the stinging blows of a stick woke him up. He was surprised to see that it was morning. It seemed to him that he'd only gone to sleep a few minutes before.

Popo had just time for a drink of water before Enrico tied two heavy cans of milk on his back. The milk was delivered each morning by Enrico's cousin, who kept Enrico's milk cows at the edge of the town.

Whack! Enrico hit Popo again, and they started off down the narrow, twisting village street.

Popo felt terrible. He knew that he had done nothing to merit the blows from the stick and that they were not required to get him to work. But his stout heart was so sad he didn't even have the spunk left to rebel and to refuse to move, as most self-respecting donkeys would have done at such an outrage to their dignity.

Enrico walked beside Popo calling, "Milk! Milk! Milk! Who wants fresh milk?"

Soon a woman came out of her house carrying a little tin cup. "I'll take a cup of milk," she said.

Enrico stopped Popo with a loud "Whoa." He took

the woman's money and poured her a cup of milk, and then they continued on their way.

"Milk! Milk! Milk! Who wants fresh milk?"

A little girl came running out of her house. She held a pitcher so she could get a pitcher of milk for her family's breakfast. She gave Enrico the money that her mother had given her for the milk.

It only took about two hours for Popo and Enrico to go through all the streets of the small town. Enrico sold all the milk.

Some of the children petted Popo, but Enrico always frowned at them so hard when they did this, that the more timid children only barely touched Popo's nose and whispered a hello in his ears. Hard-hearted Enrico didn't feel that animals were to be petted at all; he felt that they were only to work until they could work no more.

When they arrived back at Enrico's house, Enrico took the empty cans from Popo's back, and immediately Popo looked around for some food. There was a stack of corn just outside his pen.

"No you don't!" Enrico growled in a gruff voice, seeing that Popo was going to eat some of the corn. "We are going up the mountain to bring down some firewood. You can eat when we get back."

Whack! Whack! The milkman hit Popo with the stick.

"Get going, you clodhopper!"

Popo was willing to work, but he was very hungry. He shuffled sadly down the street, not looking at all like the gay and happy donkey he had once been. He knew now that Don Carlos had been a fair and pleasant master to work for, and he missed him almost as much as he missed Don Pancho and his mother. He also missed Red who always had a word of cheer or a piece of advice to

give him. Now he had nothing but the blows of a stick and a very unpleasant taskmaster.

Popo was thinking so hard he didn't watch where he was going, and as he turned around the corner of a house, he met with sudden disaster.

Crash! Plop! Thud!

Popo had bumped into a breadman carrying hot bread and sweet rolls on a long board balanced on his head. Bread and sweet rolls flew in every direction, and hungry Popo lost no time in gobbling up as many of the tasty rolls as he could reach.

"Stop! Stop! Oh, my bread, my rolls!" wailed the breadman.

"Bad donkey!" Enrico cried. Whack! Whack! He hit Popo hard with his stick. "Now look what you've done, you dunderhead!"

But Enrico was very sly, and he quickly changed his point of abuse. He didn't want to pay for all the spilled bread.

"It's all your fault," he growled at the breadman. "It's all your fault . . . you didn't look where you were going. You might have hurt my valuable donkey."

"Oh, no, it was your donkey's fault!" the breadman yelled back. He was very angry. "Look! He's already eaten six rolls. Stop him!" he insisted, and he began to pick up scattered loaves of bread and sweet rolls.

The breadman stood in front of Enrico with legs apart. "Give me my money for the wasted bread," he demanded.

The breadman was much larger than Enrico and stood very resolute and unyielding, his broad face flushed with anger. Enrico reluctantly handed over some money.

Whack! Whack! "Get up, blockhead!" he yelled at Popo. Whack! Whack! "You have already cost me all the money I made this morning on the milk!"

Higher and higher they climbed up the mountain, until they reached a big pile of wood that Enrico had cut the day before. He loaded Popo with so much firewood he looked like a walking woodpile. Popo staggered under the load of wood and could barely keep his balance as he returned down the mountain side.

When they reached the village streets, Enrico called out, "Firewood! Firewood! Who wants to buy some firewood?"

It was almost dark when all the wood had been sold, and they returned to the dirty little stable. At long last, Enrico gave Popo a few corn stalks and some water.

"Oh how my back aches," Popo groaned aloud. "I must run away," he thought to himself.

Popo felt rested and stronger the next morning, and he waited carefully for an opportunity to get away from Enrico.

The milkman came into the stable, and Whack! drove Popo outside where the heavy milk cans were waiting. When Enrico bent over to pick up one of the cans to tie it in place on Popo's back, Popo acted.

Thud! "Hee-haw! Take that!" Popo planted both of his hind feet squarely in the seat of the milkman's pants and kicked him over one of the milk cans.

The milk spilled and splashed all over Enrico. When the enraged man tried to get up, he stumbled over the other milk can and fell down again.

"Hee-haw! Hee-haw!" Popo laughed, and he showed all his strong white teeth in a big donkey grin.

Clippity clop! Clippity clop! . . . Popo ran away as fast as he could go, and he headed in the direction of the river, Don Carlos and the donkey train.

Chapter 7

The Escape

Enrico was speechless with anger when Popo ran away. The milkman caught a neighbor's horse to ride after the escaping donkey, but his neighbor, not recognizing Enrico and thinking that his horse was being stolen, gave chase after him. By the time the enraged, milk-soaked Enrico had explained to his neighbor what had happened, Popo had disappeared.

In the meantime, Popo raced with the wind! Whenever he saw anyone ahead of him, he would run to the side of the road to hide in the trees, grass or bushes, until he felt it was safe to return to the road. And then he would plunge down the trail again—ears flapping, tail swinging and hoofs flying.

Popo was very lighthearted. He was a free donkey! He stopped beside the trail to rest a few moments, but when he heard someone coming down the road, he hid behind some bushes.

Popo's heart leaped into his throat. He recognized Ramón the donkey thief! The scoundrel had a friend with him, and both were on horseback. Popo's legs trembled and his heart thumped loudly. The two men were heading for Rosa, the village that Popo had just run away from.

Why was the thief going back to Rosa? Popo wondered. Had he seen a donkey there that he wanted to steal? Was he coming back for him? Popo waited until the figures of the two men on horseback had disappeared, and then he ran as though demons were after him. He spent the night near a little spring, and he ate some grass before he hid in some bushes and went to sleep.

Zzzt! Zzzt! Zzzt!

Popo jumped to his feet, wide awake. The sun was shining bright, and it was a beautiful morning.

Zzzt! Zzzt! Zzzt!

What was that buzzing noise? Popo craned his neck this way and that, trying to locate the source of the mysterious sound. Then, in the middle of the path, between two large boulders, he saw a large ratttlesnake sunning himself.

If he bites me, I'll never see the donkey train or my mother again, he thought to himself. I'll wait until he moves and then I'll pass through, he decided. But after a while, Popo realized that the snake was enjoying the sun so much he wasn't likely to move for a long time.

Just then, he heard some noises on the trail behind him. Could that be Ramón the donkey thief returning, or Enrico the milkman? Popo was very alarmed. What was he to do?

Zzzt! Zzzt! Zzzt! The rattlesnake never moved from the center of the path in front of him.

Closer and closer came the sound of voices behind him.

Popo didn't know that the rattlesnake couldn't strike out more than a few inches unless he coiled himself up. If he had known this, he could have jumped with ease over the stretched out snake without any fear of being bitten.

Zzzt! Zzzt! Zzzt! The rattlesnake now saw the agitated Popo, and he coiled up and struck at the brown donkey. The snake missed Popo by only an inch, and he at once coiled up to strike again. The snake didn't wait to make any decisions; he knew instantly and exactly what to do.

"Here I go!" Popo said out loud. "Now or never!" He gathered all his strength for one big, mighty leap and jumped over the coiled body of the snake. Surprised by Popo's sudden, upward plunge, the rattler's aim missed the mark again. Moving slowly, the snake disappeared in a wide crevice of the boulder on the side of the path where some weeds grew.

Clippity clop! Clippity clop! Away Popo ran toward the river which was very near.

At the river there were people crossing on the ferryboat and Popo hid in some tall grass so no one could see him. Soon, some children came down the road and Popo realized that it was the children and not the donkey thief who had been behind him on the trail, when he had been delayed by the rattlesnake. He sighed a great sigh of relief.

There was a small white dog with the children, and the dog found Popo immediately.

"Go away, dog," Popo said. "Go away, I'm hiding."

"Whoof!" barked the dog. "Let's have a game of tag." He was a very friendly and jolly kind of dog.

"No! No! Go away before the children discover me and then others find out that I'm here," Popo said in desperation.

"Why are you hiding?" the white dog asked with one ear up and the other one down.

"Have you been bad, and you're running away from your master so he can't beat you?"

"No! No! Nothing like that," Popo replied. "I was stolen from my real master and sold to a very mean and wicked man. I'm trying to get away so I can return to Don Carlos," he explained. "Of course, I'd prefer to return to my former master, Don Pancho, and my mother," he added a bit wistfully.

"You can't stay out of sight forever," the dog declared with wisdom. "Someone is bound to see you sooner or later, and since you're alone, it will be finders keepers!" he warned.

"If I can get across this river, I can at least try to stay free until I can find one of my former masters," Popo insisted stoutly.

The white dog cocked his head, raised both of his ears, and considered Popo a moment. He was surely a sad looking, dirty donkey, and indeed he was a very tired donkey, but he also looked very brave and sounded very determined.

"Tipo! Tipo! Where are you?" called the children, and the boys and girls headed toward the tall grass where Popo and the white dog named Tipo were hidden from view of the ferryboat landing.

Tipo felt sorry for Popo, and he admired the donkey's brave attempt to return to his true master.

"All right, I'll go quietly," he agreed. "Safe and happy journey," he called back, as he ran out of the grass to join the children.

Popo watched the friendly dog and the children get aboard the ferryboat. "Oh my, I'm glad he didn't give me away," he said to himself in a low voice.

Popo waited and hid all day in the tall yellow and brown grass. He knew that after dark he could swim safely across the river. It was almost dusk and Popo was feeling very self-assured in getting across the river, when Ramón the rascal donkey thief and the still very angry and fuming Enrico rode up to the ferryboat landing.

Poor Popo could scarcely believe his eyes, and he froze still in his tracks, trying not to even breathe, but, of course, this was impossible. He overheard the two men ask the ferryboat man if he had seen a runaway donkey.

"No," the man answered, "I've been here all day and if there had been a donkey around here, I would have known it," he said with conviction. "There's been no runaway donkey here."

Soon all was quiet and still. The ferryboat man locked up his boat for the night and went home. But Ramón and Enrico were sure that Popo would try to backtrack and return to Don Carlos and the donkey train by the same path that he had already traveled and knew. The Mexicans often boast that their donkeys are very intelligent, and never need to be guided but once over any trail.

So the two men decided to wait in the shadows of the ferryboat landing for a while to see if Popo would show up. There was a big yellow moon, and they knew that they wouldn't have any difficulty seeing and roping the donkey from the backs of their swift horses.

Popo knew this, too, so he wisely decided to remain still until the men fell asleep. Then he would swim quietly and safely across the river. But he didn't reckon with the soft, fuzzy grass pollen that was stirring around under his nose in the damp evening air.

Ka-chew-w-w-w-w!

Popo jumped three feet in the air as a gigantic sneeze seized him. He was totally dismayed and surprised by his own untimely and unfortunate act.

"What's that?" Enrico questioned in a loud voice.

"It must be the donkey," Ramón guessed correctly. "Come on! Get on your horse! We'll have him in no time."

As the two men leaped into their saddles, Popo jumped at once into the river and began to swim with all his might and strength.

Ramón headed for the river, directly after the swimming donkey. He was already in the act of unwinding his long rope so he could lasso Popo. Enrico was rushing directly behind Ramón.

Yeow! Splash! Blub! Blub!

Ramón had guided his horse too near the half-submerged anchoring rope of the ferryboat, and his horse had become entangled in the rope, throwing Ramón over his head into the water.

Yeow! Splash! Blub! Blub!

Enrico's horse had collided with Ramón's horse, and he, too, was thrown into the water.

By the time the two men had managed to flounder back to shore and then to assist and catch their fright-

ened, squealing horses, Popo was across the river and long gone.

As he ran, Popo laughed to himself. He could just hear Enrico, in his loud voice, demanding that Ramón pay him back his money. Ramón the donkey thief would have a very hard time getting rid of the sour Enrico!

And Popo laughed and laughed as he ran, once again free as the wind. He was determined to find those whom he loved and who loved him, because he knew that was where he belonged.

Chapter 8

Out of the Frying Pan Into the Fire

A rabbit skimmed across Popo's nose and woke him up. He had slept near the rabbit's burrow home, and it was time for breakfast. Popo was very hungry. Visions of juicy corn floated past his mind's inner eye.

If his memory was correct, he had passed a small cornfield near this place when he had been led captive by Ramón the donkey thief some days before. So instead of grazing on the grass along the roadside, Popo immediately returned to the trail, looking carefully from right to left as he traveled, searching for the cornfield.

"Ah! There it is!" Popo exclaimed aloud in joy. But, oh! oh! there was a man in the center of the cornfield. Popo stood still, yet remained poised for flight. He wanted some corn, yet he knew he should hide.

Some inner force held him, then drew him, as though by an invisible, magnetic current toward the still, still figure in the cornfield.

Popo felt a mild shock when he realized that the man was not real. He didn't know it, but he was looking at a scarecrow, a stick figure clothed in old clothes and stuffed with hay, that was intended to scare off the greedy, hungry crows.

"Hee-haw! Hee-haw!" Popo laughed. "That's no man at all . . . just an old hat, a coat and a pair of pants stuffed with straw."

Popo took a bite of the straw sticking out of the scarecrow's coat sleeve. "That isn't so bad. I'll just try some more," he murmured under his breath. So he ate more and more straw, and the scarecrow got thinner and thinner; until, with a final tug, Popo pulled the scarecrow down.

"Caw! Caw! Caw! "

Popo looked up. From out of the sky, a large flock of black crows were flying down into the field to eat the corn now that the scarecrow was no longer there to frighten them away. This reminded him that corn was better than straw, and he began to eat the corn.

Popo became so intent on filling his stomach with corn that he forgot to be cautious and to watch for the owner of the cornfield. He didn't see the farmer who was running toward him and the crows with a long black gun in his hands.

Bang! Bang!

"Caw! Caw! Caw!"

"Hee-haw! Hee-haw!"

The angry farmer shot twice and then stopped to reload his gun. Both the crows and Popo got out of the cornfield as fast as wings and legs could carry them. Luckily, the shots had been wild and no one was hurt.

"That was no firecracker!" Popo exclaimed to the wind as he picked up his heels and ran with all his might down the trail.

Popo ran so fast he had no chance to observe if anyone else was on the road or not. Imagine his alarm and surprise when he realized that he had run right into the middle of a gypsy caravan!

The gypsies were immediately alert to the runaway Popo in their midst, and in a twinkling moment, a dark, bright-eyed youth had flung a rope around the runaway donkey's neck.

Popo's heart fluttered as he struggled briefly. He was no longer free, and he trotted sorrowfully behind a wagon to which the rope around his neck had been swiftly tied.

At first the gypsies loaded Popo with a canvas tent and a lot of pots and pans. They didn't know if Popo's owner was in the area or not, but they knew that a runaway donkey would be less easy to recognize beneath such a large covering.

But after a few days and when the gypsies discovered how smart Popo was, the youth named Pico, who had originally caught the brown donkey, taught him various tricks. A donkey who could do tricks was a valuable donkey.

Popo learned to stand on his hind legs and walk around; he learned to lie down and play "dead donkey;" and he learned to tell how old he was by striking the ground the correct number of times. Of course the gypsies only guessed Popo's age, and because he was such a sturdy, strong donkey, they thought he was a year older than he was.

There were twenty gypsies in the group, and they all wore bright colorful clothes. Some could sing, some could dance and some could play musical instruments.

One old man could play beautiful, gay melodies on an old, old violin which he held with tender love under his chin as he played. Several of the younger men played deep-throated guitars, and one young girl of eight played a small harp-like instrument which she held in her lap. From this harp she played very sweet, rippling music that made every heart sing.

When the gypsies put on a show in one of the villages, Popo's act was always the children's favorite. They laughed and clapped their hands to see him roll over on his back with his feet in the air as though he were indeed dead. They always admired his ability to tap with his foot on the ground how many years old he was. But the children were particularly delighted with the end of Popo's act.

He had learned to take Pico's hat and to carry it around with the brim between his teeth while the happy audience tossed coins into the crown. But all was not show, music and glamour. There were many workdays on the road.

Popo liked the bright lad Pico, but he tried to stay

clear of Pico's grandmother, who was almost as sour-faced as Enrico the milkman. She had a quick tongue and a ready stick.

One evening the old lady fixed a large kettle of bean soup, and she put a very large portion of hot green chili into the soup. Popo was curious about the bean pot, and he sniffed and sniffed along the edges of the great iron pot. Pico saw this and decided to treat Popo to a dish of the soup which he considered to be very delicious. He ladled out several large spoonfuls of the soup into an old copper bowl and gave it to the donkey as soon as it had cooled from the fire.

Popo took a large gulp of the soup, and the fiery chili burned his throat like ten lumps of live coals!

"Hee-haw! Hee-haw!"

Crash! Bang!

In his rush to get to some water, Popo kicked over the bean pot, spilling the soup, and breaking two of the tent stakes, causing a portion of the grandmother's tent to collapse. The grandmother chased Popo with a stick and never again did she trust the donkey near her camp-fire. Of course, Popo was glad to stay away from the old lady's sharp tongue and heavy stick; and never, never again would he want to try any more bean soup.

The gypsies traveled farther and farther south and farther and farther away from where Popo had last seen Don Carlos. He knew he would probably never again see the village where he was born. He sighed and sighed when he realized that if he had been content to eat some grass instead of stealing the straw man and the corn in the farmer's field, he would never have run blindly into the gypsy caravan.

Popo thought hard about this. He knew now that it was necessary to be entirely honest at all times, even when no one was looking. He knew also that it was necessary always to have presence of mind and to remember what one is about. Popo had a funny solemn look on his long face. He knew now that it was not enough to be just smart; it was necessary to be wise in this world. And Popo was beginning to learn that to be wise is to have understanding.

Gradually the villages and towns came farther and farther apart. The country became very primitive and was filled with jungles and jungle-covered mountains. There were fewer and fewer people to give shows to, and the gypsies were running out of money and food. They had never been in this part of Mexico before, and they realized that they would have to return to the more populated areas in order to live.

One day the gypsies sold Popo for a large sum of money to a very prosperous peddler named Señor García. *Señor* means mister in the Mexican language. Popo accepted this change in masters without any feeling of alarm. He had resolved to be as happy and content as possible, no matter where he was or who he was with.

He had wanted to see the world and to have adventures, and that was exactly what he was doing, Popo reminded himself, with a sly grin tugging down one corner of his lower lip. He knew now that seeing the world and having adventures meant meeting new people, seeing new things and often being in very uncomfortable circumstances as well as in pleasant ones. Popo was truly becoming very wise!

"All right, world! Here I am and here I come," he announced to everyone and to no one, as Señor García led him away.

"Hee-haw! Hee-haw! I am living the Adventure of Life, come rain or come shine," Popo declared firmly, and he was no longer gloomy or sad, but his old, radiant, and happy self again.

Chapter 9

A Parrot, a Clown and a Show

Señor García was a happy-go-lucky fellow with a smile for everyone. He was on his way to some tiny jungle villages, and he loaded Popo with candy, salt, canned food and gaily colored cloth.

In the jungles of southern Mexico, there are very few roads and so the people must either ride a horse or donkey, or else walk most of the time. Sometimes they travel by river in little wooden boats made out of tree trunks.

Popo enjoyed this new exciting country. He was

57

constantly alert to the quick movements of wild animals and the strange calls and sounds of many colorful birds. Against the deep green of leaves and fern and the deep brown of tree trunks could be seen the brilliant flash of emerald, the ruby-red and sapphire feathers of the jungle birds.

"Hee-haw! I wish my friends in the donkey train could see this part of Mexico," Popo said to his new master. Although Señor García didn't understand, he smiled pleasantly. They were on a twisting trail that followed a little river that danced merrily in and out and around the mountains.

Click! Click! Crash!

A brown deer and her little fawn leaped across the path ahead of Popo, landing in some dry, dead branches and brambles on the jungle floor. The deer had been drinking from the river, but when they had heard Popo and Señor García coming, they had leaped across the path into the jungles as quick as a bullet shot out of a gun.

The trail became steeper and steeper. Señor García stopped Popo and tightened the straps of the pack on his back. Late in the afternoon, as the orange sun dipped low in the sky, they came to a small village that overlooked a deep mountain valley.

"We'll spend the night at Doña María's," Señor García said to Popo. He was a talkative man, and he was already in the habit of explaining everything to the little donkey.

Doña María was a very important person in this village because she owned the only grocery store. The grocery store was in the front part of her home. She also sold meals and rented rooms to travelers like Señor García. She was a short, plump woman with twinkling black eyes.

As Popo and Señor García came into Doña María's front yard, someone called out "Burro! Burro!"

"Hee-haw! Hee-haw! Who wants me?" Popo asked, looking all around.

"Burro! Burro! Ha! Ha! Ha!"

Popo now saw a big green parrot, with a bright yellow head, perched on the back of a chair on Doña María's front porch.

"Burro! Burro!" the parrot repeated over and over, and the beautiful bird watched Popo closely with inquiring, roving eyes.

"Hee-haw! Hee-haw! I see you," Popo replied, and since he had never seen a parrot before, except in the jungles in the last few days, he watched the bright bird as closely as the bird watched him. Señor García laughed as he watched the bird and the donkey. The bird flew over to the porch railing and paced up and down, constantly keeping its bright, piercing eyes on Popo. The colorful bird and the brown donkey were fascinated with one another.

Señor García continued to chuckle as he led Popo around to the side of the house where he unloaded the donkey, and then gave him some water to drink. He then pulled the heavy, grain-tasseled tops of some tall grass and fed Popo the choice food.

While Señor García was doing this, a very funny looking man came up to talk to him. The man wore a red and white suit, red shoes and an odd, pointed white cap. His red shoes were also pointed and very long so that they flopped when he walked with a sound that went Flap! Flap! Flap! with every step. The funny looking man was a clown who went from village to village to put on one-man shows for the villagers. The clown's name was Pepe and he knew Señor García very well.

"Greetings, Señor García," Pepe said as he bowed deeply all the way to the ground. "Will you let me borrow your fine donkey for an hour, if I give you a ticket to my big show tonight?"

"Greetings, Pepe," Señor García replied. "What great show is it that you speak of?" Señor García loved to tease Pepe.

"The best show in all Mexico!" Pepe answered, with a wide sweeping movement of his long arms. "I'd like to ride your new donkey around the park and tell everyone about it."

"Oh, well, all right," Señor García agreed, taking the ticket. "But don't keep him too long. He's been on the trail all day, and he deserves a rest," he told the clown.

Popo had been looking at Pepe closely, observing his strange, bright clothes. He was suspicious of the clown and refused to stand still.

"Whoa!" Pepe said as he made a leaping jump in order to get on Popo's back. "Hey!" he yelled, as Popo suddenly lifted his hind feet high in the air and threw him off. "Ha! Ha! Your donkey is very quick," the clown laughed as he scrambled to his feet.

"Be good! Be good!" Señor García said, coming over to hold Popo while the clown again got on the donkey's back; but Señor García couldn't help but laugh as Popo trotted away with the clown struggling hard to keep from falling off.

There were some little boys and girls playing in the street, and when they saw the red and white clown riding Popo, they started running after them.

"Oh, we'll have a big show tonight," Pepe shouted. He looked back at the children. "Isn't that true, boys and girls?"

"Yes, it's true," they shouted back.

By this time they had gone once around the village square, and people were gathering to watch and listen.

"It will be the best show you've ever seen! Isn't that true, children?"

"Yes, it's true!" the boys and girls shouted again.

"And, everyone must buy his ticket from me before seven o'clock or they can't come in. Isn't that true, children?"

"Yes, it's true!" the children chanted, enjoying the little game with the clown.

"Yes, it's true! Yes, it's true!"

"Hee-haw! Hee-haw!" Popo brayed. By now he was having such a good time that he joined in the fun to say "Yes, it's true," in his own way.

Soon the clown rode Popo back into Doña María's yard where Señor García was waiting. As Pepe got off Popo's back, he gave him a lump of sugar and a kind pat, saying, "You are a good donkey."

Señor García put Popo in Doña María's little stable before he left to see the clown's show. Pepe had put up a small tent in the tiny town park in which to give his show. He borrowed the park benches for the people to sit on, and he collected the tickets he had sold earlier at the tent door.

The funny looking man put on his show for twenty

villagers and a group of children. Pepe had many rubber balls which he juggled in the air all at the same time, and he walked a slack rope he had tied between two iron poles. He would often pretend to fall, but he always caught himself just in time not to crash to the ground.

"Oh-h-h-h-," groaned the audience, and they caught their breath in alarm as the clown quickly caught himself in time to regain his balance.

"Ha! Ha! Ho! Ho!" the audience laughed, as the clown made monkey faces and pretended to cry when he kept sliding back down one of the iron poles.

Clip clip! Clop clop! What was that?

"Hee-haw! Hee-haw!"

There Popo stood, his head sticking in through the canvas folds of the tent entrance. The gate to his stable had opened because Señor García had failed to fasten it well. Lonesome, the little brown donkey had wandered around until the laughing from the clown's show had attracted his attention.

Señor García was embarrassed. He got up from the bench he was sitting on, intending to go over and take Popo back. But the clown was delighted with his visitor.

"Have you come to join my show? Do you have some tricks that I can't do?" he asked Popo with a wide, wide grin on his great, red-painted clown's mouth.

The boys and girls in the audience encouraged Popo to come in. "Do some tricks, little donkey. Make us laugh, burro," they shouted.

Popo responded at once. He knew what to do. He raised up on his back legs like Pico the gypsy lad had taught him to do and walked around the floor in front of everyone.

The people clapped their hands and called for more tricks. Popo lay down and rolled over on his back, putting all four legs straight up in the air.

"Look! Look! He's playing dead!" shouted the clown. "This donkey is smarter and funnier than I am," Pepe declared, and he danced and hopped around the still form of Popo, who was still playing dead.

Popo then hopped up and stamped his right forefoot on one of the flagstone rocks.

"He's telling us his age," said Señor García in a loud, excited voice. He was now as delighted with the donkey as was the clown and all the people.

Pepe jumped on Popo's back and rode around the little tent. Slyly, he reached back and tugged a little tug on Popo's tail, and Popo threw up his rear legs and spilled the clown onto the ground, which was just what the wise but funny man wanted Popo to do. It was the funniest show the clown had ever given, and he was very pleased with the brown donkey.

After the show, Señor García had to refuse over and over again to sell Popo to the clown. He liked his little donkey, and besides, where would he find another so strong and sturdy, as well as so smart, to carry his goods and merchandise? He needed Popo.

The next morning Señor García reloaded Popo, and they were ready to continue their journey.

"Where will you go from here?" Doña María asked the little peddler.

"To a village near the sea coast," he replied, "but we'll see you again in a few days when we come back through here."

"Will you bring me some coconuts?" she asked. Doña María liked coconuts better than anything.

"I certainly will," Señor García told her. "Good-by."

"Burro! Burro!" the green parrot squawked.

"Hee-haw! Hee-haw! Good-by," Popo brayed.

Chapter 10

A Monkey and Some Bees

"Tra-la-la! Tra-la-la!" sang Señor García. He had sold Doña María several bolts of cloth, as well as some of the other supplies for her store, and he was very happy. He was also happy because he especially loved this part of Mexico where life seemed more sweet and abundant then anywhere else.

They were fifty miles from the seacoast, and they traveled through country where banana trees grew wild. There were beautiful trees that looked like giant guardians planted in the earth. Some of these were tropical evergreen trees. They had a red-colored wood that gave a milk-white juice from which chicle was made. Chicle is what chewing gum is made from.

It was very lovely country indeed, and flowers grew everywhere. Popo's eyes grew rounder and rounder and larger and larger as he saw animals and birds he had never seen before. The first time he heard the grunt of a wild pig and the growl of a jaguar, which looks like a leopard, he trembled and shook.

But Señor García's happy voice soothed and reassured Popo that all was well so long as they remained on the path and minded their own business. Señor García did not carry a gun, because he was a man of peace, but he always carried a very sharp and efficient knife. In the jungle, as elsewhere, the knife is actually a necessary tool and not a weapon. Sometimes, however, when some jungle animal didn't understand that the trail was a peculiar territory of peace and neutrality, Señor García proved himself to be a very fast and trusty man with his well-balanced knife as a weapon of defense.

As they came nearer to the seacoast, the air became warmer and warmer. Señor García and Popo stopped at a tiny house where the little peddler asked for a glass of water. The smiling lady returned from her home with a glass of water and two tiny red bananas.

Señor García thanked the gracious woman. He peeled and handed one of the small, pinkish-red bananas to Popo. Popo twitched his nose and smelled the fruit carefully. He took a cautious bite and then gobbled up the rest of the sweet, mealy fruit in one gulp.

"Hee-haw! Hee-haw! Delicious!" he brayed in appreciation.

Señor García laughed. Popo had never eaten any kind of banana before, yellow or red. It was later in the morning when they arrived in a little village called Cold Water. It was named this because there was a spring of clear cold water that came right out of the mountainside near the village.

There were only ten houses in Cold Water. Señor García stopped Popo in front of one house which was also the village store.

"Anybody home?" he called out.

A short, fat man came running out. He was Señor Juan, the owner of the store. Señor Juan was even fatter than Señor García. In fact, he looked almost as wide as he was tall.

"Welcome! Welcome! Señor García. Do you have a letter for me?" he asked.

Señor García, or any other traveler who happened to be going in the same direction as the mail in these mountain villages, always carried the mail, if there was any. Señor Juan was expecting a letter from his son, Ricardo, who lived in a big city far away from the mountains.

"Yes, here's your letter," Señor García answered.

"Thank you! Thank you!" Señor Juan said, and he read his letter. His round face spread wider and wider in a great big smile as he read the news from his son. When he finished, he looked up at the waiting figure of Señor García.

"Will you stop and have lunch with me today?" he asked.

"Yes, thank you," Señor García replied. He had, of course, been waiting for the invitation, because Señor Juan always invited him to eat with him.

"I'll unload your salt, candy and canned food first," he said, as he began to untie the straps of the load on Popo's back.

"Looks like you have a new donkey," Señor Juan remarked.

"Yes, and he's a fine donkey," Señor García answered. "You should see him do tricks! He's very smart," he told the other man. "Can you sell me some corn for him?"

"Oh, I wouldn't charge you for a little corn," Señor Juan said as he openly admired Popo's sleek coat of brown hair and his strong, well-built form.

"Here!" he said, and he took a can from a small shed nearby and poured a quart of corn into a feedbag. He tied the bag around Popo's neck.

After lunch, Señor García took a little siesta, which means that he took a little nap. So Popo took a little siesta also. It's a pretty fine life, he told himself, as he opened one eye and lifted his long ears.

When Señor García woke up from his nap, he reloaded the pack on Popo's back, which was much lighter now than it had been when they had first started out.

"Will you do me a favor?" Señor Juan asked the happy peddler.

"Of course," Señor García replied. "What can I do for you?"

Señor Juan was holding a tiny cage. Inside the cage was an even tinier brown monkey with two huge round eyes.

"Please take this monkey as a gift to my uncle in the next village," Señor Juan requested. He held the cage out to Señor García who took it as though he were not certain that he really wanted to.

"Are you sure he can't get out of that cage and escape?" he asked.

"Oh, no! He's too small and weak to force the door open," Señor Juan was quick to reply. "Besides, he's a very well-mannered monkey," he said laughing.

"Look," Señor Juan said. He opened the cage, and the little monkey jumped out.

"Now watch!" the little fat man said. He set a soda water bottle, with only a few drops of liquid left in the bottom, in front of the monkey. The tiny monkey grabbed the bottle with both tiny hands, and tipping the bottle up, drank the last few drops of the sweet soda water.

"Ha! Ha! Ha!" laughed Señor García. "We'll take

him for you. He's a smart little fellow!"

Now Popo had never seen a monkey close-up before, and he eyed the little creature with some curiosity and a little suspicion. He wasn't sure just what the little animal was or what he might do.

Señor García tied the cage with the monkey inside on top of Popo's pack and said with a laugh, "All right, no monkey-shines out of you."

"Hee-haw!" Popo agreed, and off they went.

Everything was quiet on the trail, and it might have been a peaceful afternoon if Señor García hadn't seen some wild honey bees buzzing around a tree stump where they kept their honey.

There was nothing Señor García liked better than honey, and he decided to try and take some from the bees. He took some old rags he had and set them on fire and threw them right in the middle of the tree stump. He thought he could smoke the bees out long enough for him to take some of the honey.

But Señor García was wrong. The rags just didn't make enough smoke to frighten the bees away; there was just enough smoke to make them angry. As everyone knows, angry bees are dangerous bees.

"Bzzzz! Bzzzz! Bzzzz!" The bees came buzzing out of the tree trunk to find their enemy.

"Ouch!" cried Señor García, as a furious bee stung him.

"Hee-haw!" brayed Popo as an angry bee stung him, also.

"Run!" Señor García yelled, as he picked up his heels and ran as fast as his little short legs could carry him toward a nearby river.

Popo didn't need to be told to run. He had already started running with his first bee sting. He leaped over a large rock and the door of the monkey cage flew open. The tiny monkey landed on Popo's neck just as the straps of the pack on the donkey's back broke. The pack fell to the ground with a loud bang.

The frightened little monkey clung tightly to Popo's neck as the angry bees continued to buzz over their heads.

"Bzzzz! Bzzzz! Bzzzz!" sang the bees loudly.

"Hee-haw! Hee-haw!" Popo exclaimed as another and another bee stung him. He ran faster and the tiny monkey held fast to Popo's ears to keep from falling off.

After Popo had leaped over some more bushes and rocks, the monkey landed upon the donkey's head between his ears. This would have been all right, except the poor frightened monkey now had his two tiny hands over Popo's eyes, and the brown donkey couldn't see where he was going.

Swish! Swoop! Swish!

Popo shook his head back and forth, from side to side. He was trying to make the monkey take his hands away from his eyes so he could see. Like a falling brown leaf, the tiny monkey slid down Popo's neck and along his back, and just managed to grab the donkey's tail in time to keep from falling off.

Señor García had already plunged into the river, and although he was sopping wet and bee stung, he couldn't help laughing when he saw the monkey flying through the air, clinging to Popo's tail.

Splash!!! With a desperate leap, Popo joined Señor García in the river. The monkey didn't like the water and was quick to scramble up onto the donkey's back. The little animal climbed over Popo's back to sit once again on his head. He held tightly to Popo's

ears, chattering like a little magpie bird in a high scolding voice.

At the river, the bees turned around and flew back in triumph to their tree stump and their honey. Señor García and Popo came out of the water, dripping wet and aching all over from the bee stings. The bees hadn't stung the little monkey, but the tiny animal was so disturbed and upset by Popo's wild flight and jump into the river, that he was trembling all over.

Señor García soothed the monkey with a soft voice and tender hands, until gradually the monkey ceased to chatter and tremble and became quiet. Then Señor García put him back into his tiny cage.

Señor García had a small bottle of bluing in his pack, which was an old-fashioned remedy for ant and insect bites. He dabbed his and Popo's bites with the deep blue liquid until they were a strange and funny sight indeed with blue spots all over them. Of course, bluing was originally intended for the family wash to make it appear whiter and brighter, but Señor García knew all the old-time tricks and remedies when there was no better medication to be had.

It wasn't long before he had reloaded Popo with the fallen pack, and they resumed their journey. Señor García, Popo and the monkey all dried quickly in the bright, warm sunshine.

Chapter 11

Popo on a Sit-Down Strike

Señor García and Popo continued their trip through the jungles. Loud screeches and strange noises from the jungle birds and animals rang back and forth within the mysterious depths of the deep forest.

Popo began to think of all the things that had happened to him since he had been stolen from the donkey train. Don Carlos has probably another donkey to take my place, he thought, and the thought bothered him. Señor García was a good, kind man who needed him, but in the inner core of his heart, he knew that he wanted to find the donkey train again some day. Popo didn't know it, but he was growing up and beginning to feel the responsibility of what he did with his life.

Popo and Señor García stopped in a tiny jungle village to spend the night, and here Señor García delivered the small monkey to Señor Juan's uncle. This village was so small there were only four houses and no store. The houses were made of clay and straw, with only the bare earth for a floor and great, dry banana leaves for a roof.

In this part of Mexico, the jungle supplies most of the people's food, and they don't have to work hard in order to have something to eat. The people of this village were happy to see Señor García, and they all came out to greet the little peddler.

This was a very remote place and the people seldom had visitors from any distance away. They were especially glad to see the friendly Señor García and eager to talk and joke with him. He could always give them all the news of the villages he had been visiting, as well as make them laugh with his funny tales and stories.

One of the men invited Señor García to his house to eat and to spend the night. Popo was petted by the children and fed choice corn and grass. But soon all left to go inside to eat except one little boy who wanted to play some more. Popo was quietly munching some grass when he saw a woman bring out a bowl of beans and a spoon. She gave the bowl of fresh cooked beans to the little boy.

The little boy set the bowl of beans on a flat tree stump that made a perfect table, but before he could sit down to eat any of the beans, a tiny, skinny pig came running from around the house, saw the bowl of beans and gobbled them up, all in one great gulp!

This had happened so fast that the little boy had only time to open his mouth, and by the time he began to cry over his loss, the greedy pig was out of sight.

Hearing the little boy crying, his mother came to the door to see what was wrong. She saw the empty bowl.

"Oh, you greedy child!" she exclaimed. "You have already eaten all the beans," she scolded her little son. "Now you have a stomach ache from eating so fast like a pig. Come inside," she said. "I will give you something to sooth your stomach ache."

"Hee-haw! Hee-haw! Hee-haw!"

Popo tried hard to tell the woman that the beans had indeed been eaten by a real pig, and not by her little son, who had nothing to eat at all. But, of course, the woman couldn't understand donkey language, and only Popo, the hungry little boy, and the greedy pig knew the truth about where the beans went.

That night a big yellow moon shone down through the tall trees as though it were hanging overhead in the sky just for the purpose of lighting up the little village. The people came out of their houses to sit together in the strong yellow glow of the moonlight, and Señor García entertained them with all the news and happenings in the towns and villages he had passed through recently. He told of marriages and of births, and of fortunes and misfortunes.

One man strummed a guitar. It wasn't long before two other men began to play and plink their guitars also. And then everyone began to sing. They clapped their hands and tapped their toes to the rhythms of the gay music. One young couple danced for them.

When the song and dance were over, the people asked Señor García to sing for them. Señor García couldn't sing well, but he had a strong voice, and he was always willing to join in the fun of the people. Of course, Señor García privately thought that he had one of the best voices in all of Mexico.

He sang a song about a one-eyed rooster, and when

he came to the part where the rooster was supposed to crow, he stopped and looked at the children who were waiting for just this moment.

"Coo-coo-rue-coo-coo!" they chanted together, delighted with their part of the song, and they flapped their arms to imitate a crowing rooster.

In a few minutes, all the real roosters in the village began to crow. They all thought it must be morning because they had heard the children crowing like roosters.

Señor García stopped singing, and all the people laughed. The children laughed the loudest of all. They thought it was a great joke on the roosters.

"Hee-haw! Hee-haw! Hee-haw!" Popo brayed. He raised up on his hind legs to show that he enjoyed the joke too.

No one asked Señor García to sing another song, and before long everyone went to bed. All the children gave Popo a loving hug and wished him goodnight.

Señor García and Popo left the little village very early the next morning, and the people waved good-by and told them to hurry back. In the middle of the morning, they came to a deep but narrow creek. There was a very peculiar bridge across the creek that was not at all like an ordinary kind of bridge.

There were two ropes strung just above and across the water that were tied to some trees on each side of the creek. Across these two ropes were tied some boards, one after the other, to walk on. Up higher, above the boards, two more ropes were tied across the stream of water between the same trees, in order to give the person walking across the boards something to hold on to.

Popo saw at once that the two higher, hand ropes wouldn't be of any use to him if he tried to cross the shaky, swaying bridge. In fact, he didn't think the bridge was for him at all.

Señor García looked up and down stream to see if he could find a shallow place where Popo could cross, but he couldn't see such a place.

"Well, we'll just have to make the best of it, old friend," he said to Popo, tying a rope around the donkey's neck.

"There now, if you fall off the bridge, I'll hold your head above water with this rope," he explained.

"Hee-haw! No, thank you!" Popo said, and in protest, he put his ears back and sat down.

Señor García pulled and pulled on the rope and coaxed and coaxed Popo to get up, but Popo refused to move. Finally, Señor García tried to bribe Popo with a handful of corn. Popo ate the corn, but he still wouldn't budge. He didn't like the bridge, and he had no intention of trying to go across it.

Whack! Señor García hit Popo lightly with the end of the rope, but Popo just settled down more comfortably on the ground.

"Ha! Ha! Ha!" Señor García laughed, as though he

77

had just thought of something very funny. He had a fine idea. "Why didn't I think of that before?" he said aloud. He took off his shirt and tied it over Popo's eyes.

"There now! What you can't see won't hurt you," he said. "Get up!" he urged Popo.

Sure enough, Popo got to his feet and started forward. With the shirt over his eyes, he couldn't tell one direction from another. All went well until one front hoof touched the first shaky board of the rickety bridge. That was enough for Popo.

"Hee-haw!" he brayed loudly. Up went Popo on his hind feet. He spun around, jerked the rope out of Señor García's hands and started to run. As he turned, Señor García's shirt slipped off one of his eyes, and Popo could see where he was going.

"Oh my! Oh my!" Señor García wailed in distress, and he started to run after Popo.

"Oh me! Oh me!" he moaned. "Not only am I losing my donkey and my supplies, but my Sunday shirt as well. Señor García only owned the one shirt, but he always washed it every Saturday night so it would be clean for Sunday.

Finally, Popo stopped and let Señor García catch him. The little man was huffing and puffing from so much hard running. After leading Popo upstream for a while, he found a place in the stream that wasn't very deep or very swift, and both he and Popo waded across to the other side of the creek. Soon they would reach the end of the trail and reach the deep blue waters of the Pacific Ocean.

Chapter 12

Popo Enters a Donkey Race at Blue Beach

In the early afternoon of the next day, Señor García and Popo arrived at a seashore town on the Pacific Ocean. The name of the town was Blue Beach because the sandy beach along the ocean was dark bluish in color. It was a holiday, and the whole town was bustling with people. There were rooster fights, horse races and even a donkey race to entertain the people.

Señor García delivered the rest of his supplies to a merchant whose store overlooked the deep, blue beach of sand and the blue, blue water of the Pacific Ocean. After receiving his money for the supplies, he hid it away in a secret money belt. Then, taking Popo with him, he went to watch the rooster fights.

But Señor García was a tender-hearted man, and

he didn't enjoy the cruel contest between the blood-thirsty roosters. So he left the rooster fights to see the horse races. Popo was strangely excited to see the horses race. He loved the spirit of the contest. He could sense the anticipation and the thrill of winning a race, and he knew that the crowd of people around him felt this too.

After the horse races, Señor García overheard a man say that now there was to be a donkey race at the edge of the town. He thought that would be interesting, so he got on Popo's back and rode out to see the donkey race.

"Hello, Señor García," said a friendly voice. Señor García turned to see who had spoken to him, and he saw a good friend.

"Hello, Tonio," he said in surprise. "I didn't expect to see you here."

"Aren't you going to enter your fine looking donkey in the contest?" Tonio asked his friend, admiring Popo's sleek, strong build, despite his small size.

"I guess not," Señor García replied. "He's been working hard. We only arrived this afternoon, and we have to start back early tomorrow morning. He needs to rest."

"Well, that's too bad," Tonio said. "The winner will receive ten dollars, and your donkey looks faster than most of the others here." Tonio had carefully looked over all the donkeys that had been entered in the race, and he was an excellent judge of donkeys.

Of course Señor García was aware of this, and he began to consider the possibilities of entering Popo. Popo had carried only a light load that morning, since many of the supplies had already been sold before they arrived in Blue Beach. He looked silently at Popo with a questioning look in his eyes.

Popo straightened up and tried to look fresh and

lively. He wasn't very tired, and he wanted to see if he could outrun the other donkeys.

It's a great honor to have a winning donkey," Tonio encouraged Señor García.

Popo walked back and forth before Señor García, picking up his feet smartly to show how peppy and ready he was to enter the race.

Señor García's eyes sparkled at the thought of winning the race. "All right, I'll do it," he said. "Can you get a boy to ride him, Tonio?" he asked.

"Of course," Tonio replied smiling. "My cousin Pietro will ride him. Take your donkey over to get him entered in the race, and I'll go get Pietro." And Tonio left to get his cousin who was at the concession stand drinking an orange soda pop.

In a few moments, Tonio returned with his cousin Pietro, who was a slender youth about thirteen or fourteen years of age. Señor García picked up each of Popo's hoofs to examine them. He wanted to make sure there were no pebbles stuck in the donkey's feet that might cause a bruise when Popo was running.

Pietro got up on Popo's back and Popo felt very proud. He could hardly wait for the race to start. Oh! This was an adventure indeed, he thought.

Pietro rode Popo over to get in the starting line, and Señor García gave him final instructions. "Even if you are losing, don't hit my donkey with a rope, a stick or anything," he said. "Just kick him lightly with your heels." And Pietro agreed to do just as Señor García instructed him.

There were fifteen donkeys lined up for the race. There were short donkeys, long ones, gray ones, black ones, brown ones and even a spotted one. Popo stamped his hoofs impatiently. He was eager to be off. He wanted to see if he could win the race.

The man who was called a Starter gave instructions to all the riders so they would know what to do. "You are to start when I lower my hand toward the ground," he said. "Then run as far as that big tree there," and he pointed to a large tree in the distance. "Circle the tree, and come back to the finish line."

The Starter stood to one side, a little ahead of the donkeys and their riders. He held up his hand, and in his hand was a brilliant-colored scarf.

"On your mark! Get set! Go!!!"

When the Starter called "Go," he lowered the cloth in his hand in a down-sweeping gesture toward the ground.

Off went the donkeys in a cloud of dust. When the dust cleared a little, Señor García could see two donkeys in the lead—a big black one and a big gray one. Popo and the spotted donkey were neck and neck in third place.

Popo didn't know if he could catch up with the two big donkeys ahead of him or not, but he was determined to try. Pietro clung tight to the little donkey, encouraging him in a soft, musical voice. He could tell that Popo was running with all his strength and might.

Gradually, Popo gained little by little, but it didn't look as though he would ever get ahead of the black and gray donkeys. There was a lot of shouting and excitement from the people who were watching. Señor García and Tonio were calling out encouragement to Popo, but, of course, Popo couldn't hear them over the great din of voices that rose and fell.

Each of the two lead donkeys and their riders were very confident that he would win. In fact, they were over-confident. When they reached the tree, both riders failed to slow their donkeys down enough in order to make a narrow, quick turn around the tree, and they

lost time in the wide circle they had to run in order to get around the tree before starting back to the finish line.

Popo saw that this was his chance to get ahead of the black and gray donkeys, and after slowing down a bit, he made a quick small circle around the tree. When he cast a hasty glance behind him, he saw that he had out-smarted the two lead donkeys. Now he was in the lead! But as he looked ahead of him, he was stunned to see the spotted donkey in front of him. What had happened?

Popo almost stopped short in amazement. The spotted donkey hadn't been ahead of him before he made the turn around the tree, and he didn't recall the donkey going around him. Popo and the spotted donkey pounded down the home stretch with the black and gray donkeys gaining on them from the rear. Popo willed himself to push forward ahead of the spotted donkey, but as they crossed the finish line, it was the spotted donkey who was in first place by barely a nose length. Popo was second, and the two, big black and gray donkeys tied for third place.

Popo stood quietly, catching his breath, and trying to figure out how it was that the spotted donkey had gotten ahead of him. Pietro rubbed him down with a large cloth. He, too, was puzzled, but he petted and praised Popo for his fleetness, endurance and strength.

Suddenly, they became aware of loud shouting, and Señor García and Tonio were shouting the loudest of all.

"The spotted donkey cheated!" they cried. "He didn't go around the tree at all! He didn't win!"

"Disqualify the spotted donkey," the people shouted, and they were angry and shook their fists.

Sure enough, when Popo and Pietro, and the black

and gray donkeys had circled around the tree, the spotted donkey and his rider had merely turned just short of the tree. Of course, Popo and Pietro didn't know this because they were busy making the turn around the tree when it happened.

It wasn't long before the spotted donkey was disqualified by the judges. Señor García, waving his ten dollars in prize money, came running up to Popo and Pietro. Tonio was directly behind him.

"We won! We won!" Señor García shouted, and he rushed up proudly to give Popo a hug.

A man came and put a wreath of flowers around Popo's neck. Popo held his ears straight up and switched his tail as the people shouted, "Bravo! Bravo! Bravo for the winner!"

Señor García gave Pietro a dollar for riding Popo in the race. "Thank you, Pietro," he said. "You followed my instructions exactly, and you did a good job," he told the youth.

The happy boy patted Popo again, thanked Señor García, and ran off to show his friends his dollar and to tell them of his ride on Popo, the winner of the donkey race.

That night the air was filled with the sound of music as the town band played in the park. Popo enjoyed the music as he chewed contentedly on the alfalfa hay that Señor García had bought for him. He was in a clean, fine stable.

I wish Red and the other donkeys of the donkey train could have seen me win the race, Popo thought to himself. Oh, well, I'll tell them about it when I see them again. In his secret heart, Popo never gave up the idea that he would somehow be returned to the donkey train. He thought of Don Pancho and of his mother as of fond memories never to be known again.

Señor García, as the owner of the donkey who had won the donkey race, was a guest of honor at the big dance. Early the next morning, he packed his few personal belongings and made ready to leave Blue Beach. The only load Popo carried was some coconuts that Señor García had bought for Doña María and some special sea shells for another customer. After delivering these things he planned to travel northward to a large city where he could buy some very special merchandise. He wanted to get some fine lace, cloth, ribbons and jewelry.

Chapter 13

Popo to the Rescue

Doña María was happy to receive the coconuts, and she cooked a delicious lunch for Señor García. She also fed Popo some excellent corn.

Some black chickens scratched around in the grass under Popo's feet and eagerly searched for any grains of corn that fell from his mouth as he ate. The hens cackled noisily, and one bold hen even flew up on the donkey's back to perch. Popo didn't mind, he just shook the hen off and kept on eating.

Soon after lunch Señor García and Popo delivered the sea shells and then began their journey northward. Señor García was in very high spirits because Doña María had given him a big order to bring back with him when he returned from the north.

Popo lost count of time, but one day he recognized

the countryside they were traveling through as being familiar to him. He had been there before! He raised his ears straight up and tried hard to remember just where he was. They had been traveling through some very wet weather, and now the rain was pouring down hard and fast. Both Popo and Señor García wore large waterproof ponchos.

As they entered a very familiar town, Popo's memory stirred, and he remembered being there before! This was where Ramón the donkey thief had stolen him from out of the stable while Don Carlos had been away in his room.

Popo's heart beat fast. He didn't ever want to see Ramón the donkey thief again, but he would like very much to see Don Carlos and the donkey train. He thought of his friend Red. How good it would be to see him. He liked Señor García, but he missed the donkey train and his friends, even as he had once missed his mother and Don Pancho. Strange, but he no longer missed his mother and Don Pancho so much any more, although he would very much like to tell his mother all about his adventures in the world.

Popo looked carefully to the left and to the right, hoping to see his old friends once again. The rain poured down harder and harder, and it became difficult to see clearly. Señor García rode on Popo's back. Popo didn't mind the rain so much, but walking was becoming difficult, because the narrow streets of the town were filling up with swift-running water. The streets looked like little rivers. Señor García got off Popo's back so he could help guide the donkey.

"This is a small flood!" he exclaimed in concern. The water came completely over his shoes and ran through the streets in streams.

They approached the once small and shallow river

that ran through the center of the town. The stream was now swollen until it looked like a great river. The small bridge that had once crossed the stream was gone, swept away by the rising flood waters, and there was no way to cross over. There was no way to reach the stables, stores and the main part of the town that was on the other side. The stream was like a little meek mouse that had turned into a great roaring lion.

Crack! Wham! Crash! There was a great, loud sound like a clap of thunder, as a small house fell into the angry river. The swift-running water had dug out so much earth from under the foundation of the house it had toppled over into the rushing stream. Two pigs, a duck, a dog and a little boy also fell into the dangerous water along with the house.

Help! Help!" cried the boy.

The pigs, the duck and the dog swam to safety, but the little boy couldn't swim. As he floundered in the torrent, a chair floated by, and he quickly reached out and grabbed it. The chair kept him from sinking. Señor García and Popo hurried over to the edge of the river.

The boy's mother, who had just returned from a neighbor's house with some borrowed food for breakfast, heard her little son's cries for help and saw that her house had been swept away.

She dropped the parcel of food and ran to the water's edge. She was frantic with fear for the life of her son.

"Help! Help! Someone save my boy!" she screamed, as the rain continued to pour down like thick liquid sheets.

Señor García took his rope and threw it out toward the little boy, but it wasn't long enough to reach him. "I wish I could help him, but there's nothing I can do," he said in a sad voice of regret. He considered jumping into the water to try to save the boy, but he hesitated because he knew he didn't swim well.

A number of people were now running over to where the woman and Señor García and Popo stood. They were also afraid to jump into the foaming river. The mother of the little boy moaned and wailed. "Someone save my son!" she begged.

"Mother, Mother!" the boy called, as he floated swiftly past them, still clutching tightly to the buoyant chair. But no one dared to try and save him.

"Hee-haw! Hee-haw! Here I come!" Popo brayed to encourage the frightened boy. He could no longer stand by, silent and passive. He knew he had to try to save the child.

Splash! Popo jumped into the deep, raging water and swam after the boy as fast as he could.

He soon swam alongside the terrified child. With perfect trust, the boy let go of the chair to grab Popo around the neck. Then he pulled himself up and across the little brown donkey's back. He clung tightly to his rescuer's long ears.

"Hurrah! Bravo! Bravo!" shouted all the people on the bank.

Popo started swimming toward Señor García, but he was tiring fast. The boy was a heavy weight across his neck, and in his fear, the little boy's hands had slipped down to clutch Popo in an almost strangling clasp. It became harder and harder for Popo to keep from being swept down the river.

"Oh!" cried the boy's mother, as it became clear that Popo's strength had given out about ten feet from the bank. The courageous donkey was now floating downstream. But when Señor García saw this, he quickly threw out his rope, trying to drop a loop over Popo's head.

Swish! sang the rope as it swept out through the air. "Ahhhh," groaned the people as the rope just missed going over Popo's head and fell a few inches from him in the water.

"Hurrah!" the people cheered as Popo reached out and grabbed the rope between his strong teeth.

Several men helped Señor García pull Popo out of the water with the little boy still on his back and clutching the donkey's neck. The child was returned to his grateful and happy mother and was taken to a neighbor's house and wrapped in warm blankets.

It had stopped raining, and Señor García rubbed Popo well with some dry burlap sacks that a man gave him to use. As soon as Popo was warmed up and had rested a little, he got to his feet. Everyone patted him and called him a fine, brave donkey.

Many people offered to take him home and give him some good food and a warm place to spend the night. Señor García gladly accepted one of the offers, and soon Popo was in a nice warm stable eating some corn and hay.

The man and his family who were their hosts refused to accept any money for the night's lodging. They admired the brave Popo very much and could not do enough to make both Señor García and the brown donkey comfortable for the night. Popo was content and happy.

Señor García hoped that now it had stopped raining, the flood water would go down, and in the morning he would be able to get across the river and shop in the stores.

Chapter 14

A Reunion

It was a beautiful morning. All the rain clouds had disappeared, and the sky was a brilliant clear blue. The flood waters had run off, leaving many interesting puddles of water for the children to play in. The river that ran through the town was once again a gentle, narrow stream; though not so gentle or so narrow as it had been before the flood.

Señor García thanked his kind host and hostess for their generous hospitality and took Popo to one of the stables on the other side of the river. He wanted to buy a few personal things in this town, although he intended to go farther north to a certain large city for the other merchandise that he wanted. He would leave Popo in the stable while he went to shop.

As they entered the stable, Popo suddenly stopped. Sniff, Sniff—he smelled something familiar. He looked around him carefully.

"Hee-haw! Hee-haw!" he brayed. Popo was elated with what he saw. There, eating busily away on some hay, was his good friend Red, and the rest of Don Carlos' donkey train!

"Hee-haw! Hee-haw!" answered the donkeys. They were as delighted to see Popo as he was to see them, and they crowded over to sniff noses with him. This was their special way of greeting a long lost friend.

"Where have you been and what has happened to you?" Red asked Popo. He was very glad to see the little brown donkey.

"Oh, it's a long, long story and will take a good while to tell," Popo said. "First, I want to know what you are doing here!"

"We're on a return trip to pick up some of Don Pancho's sugar," Red told him. "Some changes have been made since you left. Don Carlos and Don Pancho are partners now. Don Pancho bought a half interest in the donkey train."

"Have you seen my mother?" asked Popo, who was very glad to hear this good news that Don Pancho and Don Carlos were now partners.

"Yes, and she is fine. She will be happy to know that you aren't lost any more," Red told him. "Don Pancho only uses her to ride around on now. He has bought four other donkeys who do the work on his sugar cane farm. He is becoming a rich man."

"That is good news, indeed," Popo said. He was happy to know that his old master was prospering.

In the meanwhile, Señor García and the stable owner had settled on a price for keeping Popo. As he turned to go, who should enter the stable but Don Carlos!

Don Carlos saw Popo immediately, and his face reflected both joy and dismay.

"Popo!" he shouted, throwing up his arms in surprised delight. He went over and gave the long lost donkey a big hug.

"Say, wait a minute. Let go of my donkey!" Señor García ordered with some bewilderment. He thought Don Carlos must be mad.

"Your donkey?" Don Carlos protested with indignation. "He's my donkey!" he declared firmly, and he stood up straight and tall so that he towered over the short, plump Señor García.

"How did you come by my donkey?" Don Carlos demanded to know, looking with suspicion at poor Señor García as though he were indeed a donkey thief.

"Some gypsies sold him to me," Señor García replied quickly and honestly. "Why do you ask?"

"Because Popo was stolen from me," Don Carlos explained, "although there were no gypsies around at that time that I know of," he added, still eyeing Señor García with suspicion.

"I have friends here who will vouch for my integrity," Señor García said staunchly. "Can you prove that this donkey was stolen from you?"

"Of course, I can," Don Carlos said. "Come with me to the police station." So Señor García went with Don Carlos to straighten out the matter as to who was the real owner of Popo.

While the two men were gone, Popo told his friends of his many adventures. Later, Don Carlos and Señor García returned. They had become fast friends.

Señor García went up to Popo and patted him affectionately. "Good-by, old friend, I'm sorry to lose you. I know now that you really do belong to Don Carlos, and you richly deserve to be returned to your old master and your old home," he added.

Don Carlos had told Señor García how the brave

and intelligent Popo had twice saved the donkey train. And, of course, Señor García had told Don Carlos how Popo had won the donkey race and how he had just the day before rescued and saved the little boy who had fallen into the flood water.

"Now where is the donkey you said you would sell to me?" Señor García asked Don Carlos.

"All of my donkeys are exceptional donkeys, every one," Don Carlos declared with pride. He thought a minute as he looked his donkeys over.

"Here, I'll sell you my fine black donkey there," he said, pointing to the little black donkey whose place Popo had taken when the black donkey had a lame leg. His cut had healed a long time ago, and now he was as good as new.

"He's so small you must call him Midget," Señor García said. "He looks like a five dollar donkey to me."

"Ha! Ha! Ha!" Don Carlos laughed. "I was offered twelve dollars for him yesterday, but because you had the misfortune to buy a stolen donkey, I'll let you have him for five dollars as a special favor to you."

"All right, it's a deal," agreed Señor García, who knew that he was getting a very good bargain, and he thanked Don Carlos for his generosity.

"So long, Popo. You have been a fine friend and a good worker," Señor García said sadly, patting Popo again on the head.

"Hee-haw! Hee-haw!" Popo answered, as Señor García walked away. He had been treated kindly by Señor García, and he was sorry to see him go. Still, he was glad to be back with his donkey friends, and he was looking forward to seeing his mother and telling her all about his many adventures in the great world.

"You will be in good hands," Popo said to the black donkey as Señor García led him away.

"Good-by, everybody," the black donkey brayed. "I like to travel, and I don't care who I travel with as long as my owner is good to me," he said as Señor García led him through the stable door. All the donkeys bade their black friend good-by as he left with his new master.

Don Carlos loaded all the donkeys except Popo with some bags of oranges. He had an uncle who taught school in a nearby village, and he was going to give the oranges to the children. Don Carlos jumped on Popo's back and off they went.

The sun was straight overhead and looked like a shining ball of pure white light when the donkey train came to the place where Don Carlos' uncle taught school. As they arrived in front of the schoolhouse, they heard singing.

The teacher sang, "Who likes candy?"

The children sang, "We like candy."

The teacher sang, "Who likes milk?"

The children sang, "We like milk."

"Who likes eggs?"

"We like eggs."

"Where does the candy come from?"

"From the store."

"Where does the milk come from?"

"From the cow."

"Where do the eggs come from?"

"From the chickens."

"Where do the chickens come from?"

"From the eggs."

The singing stopped because it was time for the children to be dismissed for lunch. As they left the schoolhouse, they saw the donkey train, and most of them stopped to pet their donkey friends. Don Carlos sat down to talk with his uncle.

All the boys and girls wanted to ride Popo, because he was the only donkey who didn't have a load of oranges on his back. Don Carlos let each of them ride the little brown donkey once around the schoolhouse and then gave each child an orange. In the meantime, several large boys, under Don Carlos' supervision, unloaded the bags of oranges from the backs of the other donkeys. These were Don Carlos' gift to the children.

Popo liked the children and enjoyed giving them a free ride, and all the children loved Popo. They were all having a grand time.

"Are these all the children you have in your school?" Don Carlos asked his uncle as he watched the fun.

"Oh no," his uncle replied. "All the children can't come every day because they have to help their parents raise corn and beans. But they are good children and like to come to school when they can."

Don Carlos had lunch with his uncle. But first, he asked some of the children to bring some feed for the donkey train. They also filled a large tub with water for the donkeys to drink from. Then the children left to go home for lunch. A few had brought their lunches wrapped in paper, and they sat down on the grass to eat and keep the donkeys company.

After having eaten their lunch in a little restaurant nearby, Don Carlos and his uncle returned to the schoolhouse. Don Carlos said good-by to his uncle and to the children.

There were many fine potters in the village, and Don Carlos now went to the homes of several of his potter friends. He bought a load of beautiful red pottery for the donkey train to carry. There were clay bowls covered with beautiful, colorful glazes, cooking jars and cups of all sizes to sell to the housewives of other villages.

It had been a very happy day for Don Carlos and for all the donkeys, too, and Popo knew that they were on their way back to Don Pancho's sugar cane farm and his mother. His step was quick and light as he brayed for the sheer joy of living.

"Hee-haw!"

"Hee-haw!"

Chapter 15

Homecoming

At last, the great day arrived. It was the day of homecoming! The donkey train passed the sugar cane fields, and Popo looked for his mother and Don Pancho, but he couldn't see them anywhere. He saw some strange donkeys and two men he didn't know.

"Those two men work for Don Pancho, and those are the new donkeys that he bought," Red told Popo.

Popo smelled the old smells of the familiar countryside and of the clay, sun-baked village. The special scent of the river and the yellow-tipped grass and wild flowers that grew on the river banks were pleasant to him. He recognized people and places with a quickening beat of his heart.

Soon they came around the very same bend in the road on which Popo had first seen the large cloud of dust and then the donkey train so many months ago.

Popo began to walk faster and faster; then he started to trot, almost running in his hurry to get home. When he saw his mother waiting in the shade of Don Pancho's house, he could restrain himself no longer, and he began to run, leaving the donkey train behind him. Fortunately, Don Carlos was not on his back.

"Hee-haw! Hee-haw! Is that you, Popo?" called out his mother.

"Hee-haw! Hee-haw! Yes, it's I, Mother," Popo answered, braying loudly. "I have seen the world, and I have many things to tell you."

Don Pancho came out of the house, and when he saw Popo, he threw his arms around the little donkey's neck.

"Found at last!" he exclaimed. "I am glad to see you again, Popo," the old gentleman said fondly, as he stroked the brown donkey's head. "I've heard about your being a hero. You're a fine, brave donkey. I named you well when I named you Popo."

"Hello," called out Don Carlos as he and the rest of the donkey train entered Don Pancho's yard. "I've brought you Popo, and he's been a hero several times over again since I lost him," he informed his new partner.

Don Pancho beamed; he was very proud of Popo. "Good! Good! We will celebrate and have music this evening. It isn't every day a hero returns home," he said, with a bright sparkle of delight in his dark eyes, and the two men sat down on the front porch steps to talk.

While Don Pancho and Don Carlos made plans for the evening's celebration, Popo and his mother enjoyed a nice long talk.

"Welcome home, Popo," his mother said, with a very warm smile. "What do you think of the world?

Are you glad to be home?" she asked.

"Oh, I am very glad to be home," Popo admitted. "But I like to travel with the donkey train, too," he said truthfully. "The world is a very large place, with many strange things to see and with all kinds of people," he told his mother.

"Some of the people are not to be trusted," he continued. "Some have twisted hearts and sour faces; some are dishonest, and some are cruel and cowardly; but most of the people are honest and gentle, with kind, open hearts and open faces," Popo said.

"But I love the children best of all," he summed up, "because the children are like the flowers and the grass. They are always content and happy just to belong to life."

Then Popo told his mother of the strange but interesting gypsies, of Ramón the donkey thief, of the hot and beautiful jungles; of the high, cool mountains and of the exciting, blue expanse of the Pacific Ocean. He told her of his many experiences and of the troubles as well as the delights of the adventures he had known.

"You have learned much from your adventures,

Popo," his mother told him. "Life often tests and tries us through our experiences; some of them are pleasant, and others are most difficult to endure or to master."

Popo thought of his many different experiences, and knew that his mother spoke the truth.

"I will tell you a very special secret, Popo," his mother said, "which I think, perhaps, you are beginning to learn already. At those times when there is a need to make a very important decision, and you and you alone must make that decision, get very still within yourself—very, very quiet!

"Then listen closely to what your inner heart—your own, true inner self—has to say to you. This may not be the decision or opinion that you hear outside of you, but never mind that . . .

"In the silence of your inner self, heed what your heart tells you, and make your decision, and then act on that decision in the proper course of time. In this way, the inner truth of your being becomes outer truth and reality. In this way you will know and express the truth of life. You will know peace in your heart and serenity of being."

Popo had been listening to his mother with close attention. He knew that his mother's secret was a deep and profound truth, and that she was very, very wise in the ways of life.

"Thank you, Mother," he said gratefully. "I will always remember this special secret." And Popo knew, as he spoke to her, that he never would forget. It was truly a wonderful homecoming.

All the donkeys were given alfalfa hay and corn to eat, and that night there was a big fiesta at Don Pancho's house. There was much dancing and singing in honor of the return of the hero Popo.

Popo had a long life and spent the rest of his days in contented enjoyment of life, no matter where he was. Since Don Pancho was now the partner of Don Carlos, Popo was permitted to divide his time between having rest and play at the home of Don Pancho and in working with the donkey train and Don Carlos, delivering needed goods and merchandise to the people.

And the children everywhere loved the stout, brave-hearted Popo.

OTHER QUEST BOOKS FOR CHILDREN

THE ENCHANTED HILL by Ruby L. Radford.
Illustrated by Jane A. Evans (ages 8-12)

NATURE'S MERRY-GO-ROUND by Shirley J. Nicholson.
Illustrated by Michael B. Sellon (non-fiction, ages 8-14)

**NAVAJO BIRD TALES
TOLD BY HOSTEEN CLAH CHEE**
by Franc Johnson Newcomb.
Illustrated by Na-Ton-Sa-Ka (ages 8-14)

TREASURES BEYOND THE SNOWS by Marie A. Gouffe.
Illustrated by Michael B. Sellon (ages 8-14)

ROSE-COLORED GLASSES by Ruby L. Radford.
Illustrated by Iris Weddell White (ages 4-8)

YOUR OWN LITTLE ELF by May M. Raizizun.
Illustrated by Lucille Rowland (ages 4-8)

For a complete descriptive list of all
Quest Books write to:

QUEST BOOKS
P.O. Box 270, Wheaton, Ill. 60187